W9-BOL-670

THE SNOWMAN'S PATH

BY Helena Clare Pittman

PICTURES BY Raúl Colón

Dial Books for Young Readers *New York*

NORTHPORT PUBLIC LIBRARY
NORTHPORT, NEW YORK

For Linda, and the dream
H.C.P.

To Michael and Elizier
R.C.

Published by Dial Books for Young Readers
A division of Penguin Putnam Inc.
345 Hudson Street
New York, New York 10014

Text copyright © 2000 by Helena Clare Pittman
Pictures copyright © 2000 by Raúl Colón
All rights reserved
Designed by Jane Byers Bierhorst
Printed in Hong Kong on acid-free paper
1 3 5 7 9 10 8 6 4 2

Library of Congress Cataloging-in-Publication Data

Pittman, Helena Clare.
The snowman's path : by Helena Clare Pittman ; pictures by Raúl Colón.
p. cm.
Summary : After following a magical snowman on his nightly rounds,
Nathan makes friends with him and discovers a way to make him
happy before the snowman must leave.
ISBN 0-8037-2170-6
[1.Snowmen–Fiction. 2. Friendship–Fiction.]
I. Colón, Raúl, ill. II. Title
PZ7.P689 Sn 2000 [E]–dc21 99-046930

*The full-color artwork was prepared using watercolors.
The paintings were then scratched, scraped, and
etched before colored pencils were applied.*

The houses on our street stood like soldiers in a row. Behind each was a backyard, and the alley—a narrow roadway of garages and garbage pails, and yet, another world. In late afternoon shadows my friends and I dug in the alley's potholes for pirate treasures. We rode our bikes and they became stallions. Curtained by trees and fences, the alley seemed a place where something magic could happen. One winter something did.

Shooting a basketball into the hoop on our garage one afternoon, I watched a cement truck pull up. Its barrel turned and it spit out gray paste. I returned the friendly greetings of the men who smoothed over the new concrete, and waved to them as the truck pulled away. Wet cement gleamed pink with the setting sun, as inviting as fresh clay. Looking around first, knowing I ought not to, I drew an *N* for my name, Nathan. Then I walked along the new, soft edge, leaving a trail of footprints.

As evening fell and the moon rose, those steps looked mysterious—as if someone else could have left them, maybe a knight, or a pirate. I let my imagination play tricks until my mother called me for supper.

The next night it snowed. When I carried out the garbage, the footprints caught me by surprise. They were frosted, bathed by moonlight, leading into the shadows of the alley. Maybe a snowman had left them, I thought.

The wind sighed past the trees as I got ready for bed. Through the curtains I could see the shimmering path. Then something white flashed above our garage.

At first I thought it was a car. But there was something about the glow that made my heart beat fast.

Suddenly I saw the snowman, moving between the garage and the Rose of Sharon bush in our backyard. He was a little taller than me, and sturdy. I stayed awake to watch until my eyelids drooped.

The night after that he sat on the fence, gazing at the moon. He climbed a street lamp and vaulted onto the garage roof. I could hear him laughing. I put on my robe and crept outside. He leaped into the snow.

I could see him two garages ahead. The night was lit with his glow. He stopped and turned. I ducked out of sight. He waited and so did I. He seemed to listen, then continued on his way, now and then shooting a glance over his shoulder. I stayed in the shadows. When he moved, I moved. When he stopped, I stopped. Then I stumbled against a garbage can. He disappeared behind a tree. I pulled my robe around me, trying to stay warm. But he'd heard me, and my teeth were chattering. So I walked home.

The next night I waited near the garage. I heard a gate swing open. I saw him steal across a backyard where a jungle gym stood. He rode the swings, tumbled between rings and bars. Chuckling, he sped down the slide. My nose was running. My feet were frozen.

After that I wore my winter coat. I put on heavy socks and boots. I hid in the shadows while the snowman hopped garage roofs, tossing snow. I watched him leap garbage cans, tumble down snowbanks, moving like an acrobat.

Every night when the clock read twelve, I slipped out
the side door. I crouched behind fences while he looked into
windows, searching for something. Sometimes he turned
suddenly, as if he knew someone was there.

One moonlit night I heard the snowman singing, a sad
duet with the wind. A dim glow hung over the snow near the
garage. I filled a bag with cookies and crossed the backyard.
Gathering my courage, I stepped out of the shadows. My
heart jumped as our eyes met. He seemed startled, about to
run away.

"Wait!" I cried. I held out the bag of cookies. The
snowman looked at me with soft, prune eyes.

"Please don't go," I said.

He sat down. All I could do was stammer my name. "I'm named after my grandfather," I added, to his silence.

Then he spoke. "Nathan," he repeated, nodding.

He smiled, but those prune eyes were sad. He told me he had no name. He pointed to the stars when I asked him where he had come from. I asked if I could call him Sky. That cheered him up.

We ate cookies. We watched the dome of stars turning slowly above. I told him that we'd come from Ohio. He told me he had formed on the wind. He said someone had built him, then forgotten he was there. So he went away. He wandered the yards and alleys, moving north to keep from melting. Alone.

After that I visited him every night. We played in the snow. We talked. I told him about books I'd read. He talked about climbing clouds and drifting with snowflakes. I said that ships were my favorite thing. "And pirates," I said.

He said he loved the cold wind. "And blizzards!" he added. "You ought to see the sunrise—I mean from the other side! Up there!" he said, pointing. "Beautiful, Nathan!"

Sometimes we didn't talk at all. We shared snacks, hot chocolate for me, sherbet for the snowman, the sounds of the night. I got used to the cold. Sitting with Sky, I was warm.

"When I grow up, I'd like to be a scientist," I said one night. Then I asked him what he wanted most.

"I want to stay cold," he answered. "I guess that's all." He shrugged and looked up at the moon. Then he smiled that sad smile. I wished I could do something. Something that would make him happy.

The wind stirred and clouds rolled in. "You're shivering, Nathan," he said.

"I don't mind," I answered through chattering teeth.

He took the scarf he was wearing and shook out the snow. Then he tucked it around my collar. He touched my chin and smiled. My face must have felt warm, because he drew back.

We talked some more, then said good night. Halfway across the backyard I stopped. "Sky?" I said.

He nodded and waved.

"Sleep well," I called.

I hugged the scarf around me and went inside. Later, as snow began to fall, I heard the snowman whistling a tune, sweet yet sad. He needed someone. Someone—like him.

In the morning the drifts were three feet deep. I put on my boots and went outside. I knew what I was going to do.

I went to work under the maple tree, packing a base and rolling the head. I made her tall, round, and graceful. I found a feathered hat and a woolen shawl in a bag of clothes my parents were giving away. I got a box of prunes and a carrot, and I snapped some branches.

At last the snow woman stood there, her feathered hat dipping slightly over one prune eye. She was beautiful.

I laid the snowman's scarf
at her feet and went inside.

When I looked out the
window during the night, I
wasn't surprised to see that the
place under the maple tree was
empty. Reflected moonlight
flickered in the alley. They were
dancing.

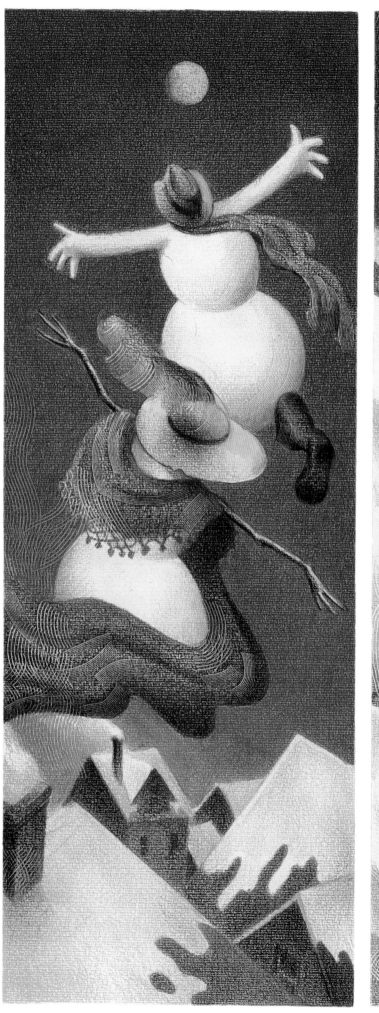

For several nights I
heard their soft laughter,
spotted them skipping
across roofs, tumbling over
snow piles and garbage cans,
together. They glowed.

One night I heard someone tapping at my window. It was Sky. The snow woman stood under the tree, where they'd first met. She was waiting for him.

"Spring is coming, Nathan," the snowman said. "I have to go, have to keep moving north."

I looked at the snow woman. She smiled. "Thank you, Nathan," she said softly.

"She's wonderful," said the snowman. "My better half."

Then he put his hand to my cheek. I could feel the drop of melted snow where his touch had been. I struggled not to cry.

"Take good care, Nathan," he said, looking into my eyes. "And stay warm!" Then he smiled, took the snow woman's hand, and helped her to the roof.

"Nathan!" he called. "One day it will happen to you!" They waved, then were gone in a gust of wind.

I still dream of them, think I hear them sometimes, when snow flies. The footprints are still there, though smaller than my feet are now. They still catch me by surprise, pointing into the alley, gleaming under the moon.

And sometimes, if I really listen, I can almost hear a voice calling "Nathan!" when the wind blows.